D0204085

Annie Bananie and the People's Court

Leah Komaiko

illustrated by
Abby Carter

Delacorte Press

Published by
Delacorte Press
Bantam Doubleday Dell Publishing Group, Inc.
1540 Broadway
New York, New York 10036

Text copyright © 1998 by Leah Komaiko
Illustrations copyright © 1998 by Abby Carter

Library of Congress Cataloging-in-Publication Data

Komaiko, Leah.
    Annie Bananie and the people's court / Leah Komaiko ;
illustrated by Abby Carter.
        p.   cm.
    Summary: When her cantankerous neighbor takes Libby's best friend, Annie Bananie, to court, Libby has to appear as a witness and tell the truth even if it gets her into trouble.
    ISBN 0-385-32115-5
    [1. Best friends—Fiction. 2. Friendship—Fiction. 3. Neighbors—Fiction.] I. Carter, Abby, ill. II. Title.
PZ7.K8347Ak   1998
[Fic]—dc21   97-29422
                                                              CIP
                                                              AC

The text of this book is set in 17-point Perpetua.
Manufactured in the United States of America
February 1998
10   9   8   7   6   5   4   3   2   1
BVG

For the Dream Team:
Craig Virden, Edite Kroll,
and Lawrence David

Chapter

1

"I am now the only person on this planet who doesn't have a dog," Libby Johnson said as she ran into her house. "I just found out the Bowers got a poodle!"

"The Bowers aren't from this planet," Mrs. Johnson said, smiling.

"What are the Bow-wows?" Grandma Gert asked. Grandma Gert was partly deaf. Nobody knew from one minute to the next what she could hear or not hear.

"Not the Bow-wows, Grandma," Libby said, giggling. "The Bowers. You know, the people who live next door."

"Aggh," Grandma Gert said. "The new

1

crazy-in-the-head neighbors. What did they do this time?"

"Nothing, I hope," Mrs. Johnson said. "You didn't go over there to pet their dog, did you, Cookie Pie?" she asked Libby.

"Don't be ridiculous, Mommy," Libby said. "I just talked to the dog. I didn't even cross the line onto their sidewalk. I wanted to rescue that poor puppy, but I wasn't about to risk my life doing it."

"Good," Mrs. Johnson said. "I want you to be alive when we eat our lunch."

"Is it time to eat now?" Libby asked. "I've got my club meeting at one-thirty. Remember?"

"How could I forget, Madam President?" Mrs. Johnson said. "Will you call your big brother to order?"

"Carl!" Libby yelled to her brother. Carl was playing the piano. Carl was always playing the piano.

"Waaa," Libby's baby brother, Daniel, screamed in his high chair.

"Time to eat, Carl," Libby yelled louder. "What are you, deaf?"

"Aggh, Libby," Grandma Gert said, holding her ears.

Mr. Johnson sat in his chair. "Let's eat."

"Good idea," Carl said, coming to the table and reaching for the potatoes.

"Wait!" Grandma Gert grabbed Carl's hand.

"Daddy, you'll never guess what I saw at the Bowers' today," Libby said.

"Let's forget about the Bowers and have a moment of silence before we eat. I hear peace and quiet is good for you."

Suddenly there was a loud banging of pots and pans outside the window.

"Lovely," Mr. Johnson said. "The Bowers want to have another one of their special conversations with us."

3

"What do we do this time?" Carl asked.

"I know," Libby said to Carl. "You could go promise the Bowers you'll never play the piano again as long as you live. Maybe you're just giving them a headache."

"That's a good idea," Carl said to Libby. "And you can come with me and promise you'll never leave the house without a bag over your head. Maybe you're just giving them a stomachache."

"Never mind," Mr. Johnson said. "I don't want anyone going over there. We all know there's no sense in talking to those people."

"Hey, Johnson," Mr. Bower yelled from his house. "Keep your daughter away from my dog. She tried to kidnap him. That's breaking the law, you know."

"They got a dog?" Carl asked.

"That's what I was trying to tell you, Daddy," Libby said.

"Did you hear me, Johnson?" Mr. Bower called again louder. "I've got proof. Your daughter dropped a stone on my lawn. Ask her. I've got it right here. It's evidence.''

''Did you lose a stone, Libby?'' Carl asked, laughing.

''I think Bower lost his marbles,'' Mrs. Johnson said. She giggled.

''Let's enjoy our lunch,'' Mr. Johnson said. ''Just ignore them. They'll stop.''

''Aggh,'' Grandma Gert said, helping herself to the potatoes. ''What's everybody waiting for?''

Right then Grandma Gert couldn't hear a thing. Then Annie Bananie and her dog, Boris, came up the walkway. Grandma Gert heard Boris's tags jingling on his collar. Grandma Gert hated dogs.

''Tell the Bananie girl if that dog comes in this house I'll flush him down the toilet,'' Grandma Gert said to Libby.

''She knows,'' Libby said, jumping up from her chair. ''Can I be excused?''

''I don't like it when you eat and run,

Cookie Pie," Mrs. Johnson said. "It's not healthy."

"But running is healthy for you," Libby said, kissing her mother good-bye.

"Not for me." Grandma Gert laughed. "If I ran from here to the Bowers' house, I'd drop dead of a heart attack."

Annie Bananie, Libby, and Boris ran down the sidewalk. The Bowers banged their pots and pans.

"Don't stop until we're far away from the nuthouse," Libby said to Annie.

"Why don't the Bowers just ring your doorbell if they want to talk to you?" Annie Bananie asked.

"Because that's what normal people do," Libby said. "And they're not normal."

"I wish they'd come out of their house," Annie said. "I just want to see what those people look like!"

"Take my word for it," Libby said.

"You've never seen anybody so weird in your life."

"Neigh," Nina Blaskewitz called from her doorway.

"I take that back," Libby said.

Nina galloped as fast as she could. Her hair flew in her face like a greasy old mane. "Hi giddyup, wait up!" she called.

"Hi giddyup, hurry up!" Annie Bananie called back. "It's time to start the meeting."

"Meow, here I am!" Bonnie Baker called, prancing down her driveway. "Purrrrfect kitty! You can't start the meeting without me!"

"Of course not," Libby mumbled.

"Meow." Annie Bananie laughed.

"Oink, you guys," Debbie Nash called from her bicycle. She pedaled fast. "What are we going to do today?" Then she stopped and listened. "What's that noise?" she asked.

"Oh my gosh, meow!" Bonnie laughed.

"Listen! The Bowers are going pots-and-pans psycho again."

"I have an idea," Annie Bananie said. "Let's go over to the Bowers' for our meeting today. We can ask them politely to stop making all that noise."

"No way," Libby said. "I'm the president. I say we should just ignore them. They'll stop. That's what my dad says."

"Meow." Bonnie hissed at Libby. "You don't have to go over to the Bowers' house. Annie Bananie and I will go."

"You're not afraid?" Annie Bananie asked, smiling at Bonnie.

"Don't be ridiculous," Bonnie purred.

"Neigh," Nina said, trotting backward. "They're only people."

"Oink," Debbie said, and pushed her glasses up on her nose. "They could be like people in a story I read. They stole kids and locked them in their basement. Do the Bowers have a basement, Libby?"

8

"How do I know?" Libby asked. "I've never gone inside their house. And I don't want to go now. Believe me, it's not that I'm afraid. The police had to come once before, and even they say we should stay away from the Bowers. Besides, my parents would kill me."

"Come on, Libby," Annie Bananie said. "You won't get into trouble. I promise. All we'll do is go and ring their doorbell. Maybe they just want company."

"And what are you going to say if somebody answers the door?" Libby asked.

Everybody looked at Libby. Nobody had thought of that. Libby smiled. That was why she was president.

"I'll give you a hint," Libby said. "I saw that the Bowers just got a fluffy little poodle. You can say you just stopped over to introduce their dog to Boris."

"You're a genius, Libby!" Annie Bananie said.

9

"Meow, you're a big baby." Bonnie hissed at Libby. "Come on, Annie. I know exactly what to say."

Bonnie and Annie Bananie walked like cats up the Bowers' sidewalk and to their front door. Boris walked right behind them. Bonnie rang the doorbell. The banging pots and pans stopped. Libby, Nina, and Debbie hid behind a tree. The door slowly opened. Annie Bananie turned to wave to Libby. When she turned back, Bonnie was running away.

Chapter
2

"What do you want?" Mr. Bower said, peering out his door. He glared at Annie Bananie.

Annie couldn't stop looking at Mr. Bower. He had sad eyes like a basset hound. His hair was thick and shiny like the hair on a doll.

"My name is Annie Bananie," Annie said in her friendliest voice. "I'm sort of new here. I live across the street. I just thought I should say hello."

"I'm not interested in visitors," Mr. Bower said, looking at Boris. Mr. Bower started to close the door. Annie could see inside the Bowers' house. All the curtains

12

were closed. A little poodle ran to the door and hid between Mr. Bower's legs. Boris wagged his tail and barked. The poodle cried and ran away inside the house.

"Now look what you've made him do," Mr. Bower said.

"Quiet, Boris!" Annie commanded. "Please don't be afraid of Boris," she told Mr. Bower. "He's friendly. Maybe Boris and your dog could be dog friends. They could have a play date. What's your dog's name?"

"Mother!" Mr. Bower called.

Annie saw Mrs. Bower coming to the door. She had big thick glasses and it looked like she could hardly see out of them.

"Who's there, Father?" she called.

"Hello," Annie called, still using her friendliest voice. "You must be Mrs. Bower. I'm Annie Bananie."

"You and your dog are standing on private property," Mr. Bower said to Annie. Then he closed the door.

For a moment Annie Bananie just stood there.

"Come on, Annie!" Libby said in her loudest whisper. "Hustle! Hustle!"

"I can't believe it," Annie said as she ran down the Bowers' driveway. "They don't like me."

"I told you," Libby said. "Quick! Let's get out of here."

"Oink," Debbie said. "You're lucky he didn't put a curse on you!"

"Neigh," Nina said.

"Meow." Bonnie sprang out from Libby's bushes. Then she fell on the lawn laughing. "That was hilarious," she said. "I saw the whole thing."

"Real funny," Libby said to Bonnie. "Nice friend. You're a bigger baby than my baby brother!"

"Hisssss." Bonnie shot her arm out at Libby like a cat about to scratch. "At least I wasn't the one afraid to go ring the doorbell.

14

That's more than I can say for you. Besides"—she smiled at Annie—"it was just a
joke. I thought you'd think it was funny. Do
you hate me for life?"

"Longer," Libby mumbled.

"Neigh." Nina trotted around Annie
Bananie and Boris. "You're the bravest," she
said.

"It wasn't so bad," Annie Bananie said
proudly. "I told you, Libby. I bet I could get
Mrs. Bower to be my friend."

"Lucky you," Libby said, looking over at
her house. "Let's get out of here."

"Follow me and Boris," Annie called.
"See, I told you we wouldn't get into trouble,
Libby."

Just then a police car turned down Barry
Avenue with its lights flashing. It pulled into
the Bowers' driveway.

"There she is, Officer!" Mr. Bower called,
running out of his house. "That's the one
with the dog! I want her under arrest!"

Chapter
3

"Exactly what is the charge?" the policeman asked Mr. Bower.

"Attempted robbery," Mr. Bower said. "She came right to my house. When I opened the door, she looked inside. That's what burglars do, you know. They look around to see what things they should come back to steal later."

"I'm not a thief," Annie Bananie said, pulling Boris closer to her.

"That's another thing, Officer," Mr. Bower said, waving his arms at Boris. "She brings a killer animal with her. She brought him to tear Weenie apart."

"What's Weenie?" the policeman asked.

"Our dog!" Mr. Bower said.

"Well, nobody seems to be hurt," the policeman said. Just then Libby's parents came out of their house.

"Oh, hello, Officer," Mr. Johnson said.

"I'm sorry to have to bother you folks again," the policeman said. "Your neighbor here says the girls were causing trouble."

"We didn't do anything wrong," Libby said. "We just knocked on the door, that's all."

"Oh, really, Cookie Pie?" Mr. Johnson said, looking at Libby.

"I did it," Annie Bananie said. "It was my idea. I just wanted to be friendly, that's all."

"Meow," Bonnie said. "I didn't do anything. I didn't even see anything!" She ran toward her house.

"Neigh," Nina said, shaking her head from side to side. Then she galloped home as fast as she could.

"Excuse me, Mr. Policeman," Debbie said. "Does Annie Bananie have to go down to the station?"

"No." The policeman smiled. "She's not under arrest. I just have to write up a report. Sorry about this, folks," he said to the Johnsons. "You know, it's just the rules."

"What about me?" Mr. Bower asked.

"I think you're safe, sir," the policeman said, petting Boris good-bye. "But I suggest you girls stay away from the Bowers. And keep your dog away, too."

"Oh, they will," Mrs. Johnson said.

"You girls take Boris home," Mr. Johnson said.

Libby, Annie Bananie, and Boris ran down the street. Debbie pedaled her bicycle fast behind them.

Grandma Gert walked out of the Johnsons' house.

"Those kids were disturbing the peace,"

19

Mr. Bower called as the police car drove away. "I have rights!"

"So do we," Mrs. Johnson shouted.

"Come on, Gert," Mr. Johnson said. "Let's all go back inside."

"We're a peaceful family," Mr. Bower hollered. "I'm warning you, Johnson, stay away from me!"

Grandma Gert walked right up to the edge of Mr. Bower's lawn. "And I'm warning you, Bow-wow," she said, shaking her finger. "You stay away from me!"

Chapter

4

"*Brringgg!*" The school bell rang when it was time to go home on Monday. Annie Bananie jumped up.

"No stampedes today, cowpokes," Mrs. Liebling said. "You're leaving school. Nobody here is breaking out of jail."

"I am," Eddie Armstrong said, scratching his head.

"You know what, Mrs. Liebling?" Bonnie said, looking at Annie. "Somebody here *almost* had to break out of jail yesterday."

"But Bonnie is the one who should have gone to jail first," Debbie said.

"What are you cowgirls talking about?"

21

Mrs. Liebling asked, laughing. "Save your imagination for your homework. Go on, I'll see you tomorrow." She closed the door behind them.

"Hisssss." Bonnie shot her arm out at Debbie.

"You're going to jail, Cat Woman?" Eddie asked. "What for? Armed robbery?" Eddie scratched his head. Dandruff fell out of his hair and onto his shoulders. He piled some of the dandruff on his finger and then licked it.

"Get a life, Snowman," Bonnie hissed. "Don't you know a joke when you hear one? Do I look like a criminal to you?"

"A fugitive!" Calvin said, jumping away from Bonnie. "Whoa!"

"Neigh!" Nina said.

Annie Bananie and Libby ran ahead across the playground.

"Hi giddyup, wait up!" Nina called.

"Oink," Debbie said, running after Nina.

"Hisssss." Bonnie tried to chase Debbie.

"Why can't you ever keep your big snout shut?"

"What about you, Bonnie?" Annie Bananie said, laughing. "You were the one who had to say something to Mrs. Liebling in the first place."

"You were the one who had to start all the trouble in the first place," Bonnie said.

"I didn't start any trouble," Annie Bananie said.

"Nice friend," Libby said to Bonnie.

"Whatever," Bonnie said. "You two can be best friends in prison. I want to go to college one day. You can't go to college if you have a police record." Bonnie purred and walked up her driveway.

"I don't have a police record," Annie Bananie said. "Come on, you guys, let's go to Libby's. Maybe we'll even see the Bowers!"

"Neigh," Nina said. "I have to practice my dressage."

"I think I have to go with my mom," Debbie said. "But if I get back fast enough I'll come over."

Libby and Annie Bananie walked together.

"I can't believe the Bowers didn't like me," Annie said, looking at their house. "Maybe they'll like me better today!"

"No way," Libby said. "I mean it." Just then she looked up and saw Mr. Bower peeking out behind the curtains of an upstairs window. "Don't look now," Libby said to Annie.

When Annie Bananie looked up, she saw the curtains close. "He's spying on us," she said.

"Yeah, right," Libby said. Then she saw Mrs. Bower standing in another window. "Oh my gosh!" Libby giggled. "Let's get out of here. This is too weird. I think Mrs. Bower is looking right at me."

"Hello, Mrs. Bower," Annie Bananie called, waving. The curtain closed quickly. "Come on." Annie laughed and pulled Libby's arm. "She wants us to come over!

How would you like to be stuck in that house with Mr. Bower? She's sending us a signal. She's saying, 'Come over for tea.' ''

"The *t* stands for *terror*," Libby said. "You can go over there by yourself if you want."

"Never mind," Annie said. "Let's just go play in your backyard."

"I don't want to get into trouble today, Annie," Libby said. "I mean it. My parents will have a cow!"

"How can we get into trouble?" Annie asked. "We're just going to play badminton on your property. We're not going to break any law."

"Okay," Libby said, getting the rackets. She served the first birdie to Annie. When Libby looked over at the Bowers' house, Mr. Bower was spying on her. "Look!" Libby cried.

"Let me see," Annie Bananie said, running to Libby's side of the net. But by the time she got there, Mr. Bower was gone.

"Go back to your side," Libby said. This time Libby saw Mrs. Bower in the window.

Annie ran again to Libby's side of the net. When Annie Bananie looked up this time, Mrs. Bower was in the window with Weenie.

"I spy!" Annie called, laughing.

"Shhh!" Libby said.

Annie hit the birdie hard over the net. The birdie sailed past Libby, over the bushes, and right onto the Bowers' lawn.

"Great," Libby said.

"Do you want me to go get it?" Annie asked, starting for the bushes.

"It's just a birdie," Libby said. "Are you crazy?"

"Get that thing off my lawn," Libby heard Mr. Bower call.

"If we're not going to save the birdie, we should at least rescue that poor poodle," Annie said to Libby. "And Mrs. Bower, too!"

"I'm not joking. We're getting out of here!" Libby said, leaving the yard.

"Mother!" Annie Bananie shouted, pretending she was calling Mrs. Bower. Then Annie followed Libby to her house.

Inside, Carl was banging on the piano. Grandma Gert was half asleep at the kitchen table.

"Hi, Grandma," Libby said as loud as she could without yelling. "I'm going to Annie Bananie's to ride bikes. Okay?"

"You're going to Annie Bananie's to rob banks," Grandma Gert said. "I'll tell your mother. But you stay away from the Bowers." Grandma Gert opened one eye. "Do you hear me?"

"Yes, Grandma," Libby said. "We'll stay away. I promise."

Chapter 5

"If you want to ride bikes, you have to heel," Annie Bananie said to Boris. "And you have to wear your best bandanna." She tied the bandanna around Boris's neck. Then she reached for her backpack.

"Oh my gosh," she said. "I left my backpack at your house."

"Let's get it later," Libby said.

"Boris needs his chew bone," Annie Bananie said. "It's in my backpack. He won't heel without his chew bone and his bandanna. Don't worry. He doesn't have to come in your house. I left the backpack in your backyard. Your grandma won't even see him."

"I'm not so worried about my grandma," Libby said. "I have a bad feeling the Bowers are going to be out there."

"So what?" Annie said, laughing. "We're just going to go in the yard and then out again. If they try to kidnap us, I'll yell for your grandma. She'll run and rescue us."

"Yeah, right," Libby said, following Annie. "If my grandmother runs, she'll drop dead of a heart attack."

Annie pedaled straight for her backpack. Boris headed straight for the bushes. He sniffed. Then he sniffed some more.

"Boris, heel!" Annie said.

"Boris, let's go!" Libby called.

Just then Libby saw what Boris saw through the bushes. Weenie was out on the Bowers' lawn. Boris barked. Before Annie could stop him, Boris ran through the bushes.

"Get away!" Mr. Bower yelled as he ran

out of his house toward Boris. "Weenie, go poo-poo!" Mr. Bower commanded. "Go poo-poo!"

Weenie yelped. Then he chased Boris around the yard.

"Mother!" Mr. Bower yelled. "Bring me a stick or something, quick! I've got to hit this dog before he attacks Weenie!"

Annie Bananie dropped her bike. She ran through the bushes into the Bowers' yard.

"No!" Libby yelled after her.

"Boris, heel!" Annie yelled. Weenie chased Boris in a circle. Annie Bananie tried to catch Boris. She ended up standing face-to-face with Mr. Bower.

"I'm really sorry, Mr. Bower," Annie said. "He's usually never this bad. But I don't ever hit him."

"Get him out of here before he goes poo-poo on my property," Mr. Bower said, "or I'll have my wife call the police."

Annie saw Mrs. Bower in the window.

"Come on, Boris," Annie said, grabbing him by his collar. "Please don't call the police," she said. "Boris was just trying to be friendly. He won't ever do it again. It was nice to meet you again." Annie ran back toward Libby's house, pulling Boris with her. Boris's best bandanna was lying on the Bowers' lawn.

"Let's go," Annie called to Libby.

"No!" Libby said. "Don't go that way. We've got to go through the alley. My grandma or somebody might see us if we go past the front of my house. But nobody ever goes through the alley."

"Okay, okay," Annie Bananie said. "Don't be such a worrywart. We didn't do anything wrong."

Annie Bananie, Libby, and Boris started through the alley. The alley was mostly rocks and stones, and it was hard to pedal their bikes. When they had almost reached the end of the alley, Libby heard something coming up behind them. She looked and saw Mr. Bower. He was right behind them in his beige car.

"Oh my gosh!" Annie said. "I thought you said nobody ever goes in this alley!"

"Don't be such a worrywart," Libby said, trying to laugh.

"Hey, Mr. Bower," Annie Bananie yelled. "Want to play tag?"

"Annie!" Libby said. "Why did you say that?"

"I don't know," Annie Bananie said. "It just came out of my mouth."

Libby followed Boris and Annie Bananie right out of the alley and turned right. Mr. Bower turned right, too.

"Which way should I go?" Annie asked.

"Now that you've asked him to play with us? Go straight," Libby answered. "He'll probably turn down our street."

Libby looked behind her. Mr. Bower wasn't turning. He was driving slowly behind them. Libby pedaled fast. She followed Annie

Bananie up onto the sidewalk. Mr. Bower drove right beside them on the street.

"Don't look at him," Libby said. "Just ignore him."

"Don't look now, Libby," Annie said, whispering, "but I think Mr. Bower is wearing a wig. I bet that's not real hair."

"Come on." Libby laughed. Then she pumped her pedals as fast as she could. Finally Mr. Bower turned and drove away. Libby and Annie Bananie stopped. Boris was panting hard. Annie looked down at his neck.

"Oh my gosh," she said. "Boris's best bandanna!"

"We should go back and find it," Libby said.

"Maybe we should go back and tell somebody," Annie said as she tried to catch her breath.

"Tell them what?" Libby asked. "That Boris lost his bandanna?"

"No, that Bower tried to run us over," Annie Bananie said.

"We're safe now," Libby said. "Besides, what are we going to say? That we told Bower to chase us?"

"*I* told him to chase us," Annie said.

"Yeah, but *I* promised we wouldn't even go near the Bowers', remember?" Libby said. "Let's just go look for Boris's bandanna. Let's not tell anybody what happened. I don't want to get into any more trouble. Promise?"

"Okay," Annie said. "I promise. We won't tell anybody."

Chapter 6

"Stop playing! Are you deaf?" Libby yelled at Carl a few days later. Carl was banging on the piano. He couldn't hear a word. Libby ran to the door. Somebody was knocking, but she could hardly hear them. She opened the door and saw Annie Bananie and her mother, Joy. There was also a man in a uniform. He wore a shiny badge that said SHERIFF on it.

"I tried to call you on the phone, but nobody answered," Annie said.

Libby stared at the man. Her heart was pounding.

"This is Sheriff Bridges. He just came to our house," Annie said. "Boris loves him."

"Hello, young lady," the sheriff said to Libby. "Is your mother or father home?"

"I'm not sure," Libby said, looking at Annie Bananie. "But I didn't do anything."

"We know, honey," Annie's mom said to Libby. "Don't worry. You're not in any trouble."

"But *I* am," Annie Bananie said, trying not to smile. "My mom and I have to go to court."

"She didn't do anything, I promise!" Libby said to the sheriff.

Mrs. Johnson walked into the room. "Hello, Joy," she said to Annie's mother. "What's the matter?"

"Sheriff Bridges just served us with this," Annie's mother said, handing a paper to Mrs. Johnson. Libby watched her mother's eyes while she was reading.

"It's a court order," the sheriff said. "It's against Annie Bananie and her mother, as Annie's legal guardian. It was filed by your neighbors, the Bowers."

"For what?" Mrs. Johnson said. "What could Annie possibly have done?"

"It says she went to the Bowers' with the intent to rob and steal," the sheriff said. "It says she brought Boris over to their house with the intent to hurt their dog. And finally it says Annie Bananie brought her dog's excrement to the Bowers' and dumped it on their lawn."

"She didn't do any of that," Libby said. "What's excrement?"

"Turds," Annie said, giggling.

"Oh, for goodness' sake," Mrs. Johnson said. "Those people are nuts!"

"They may be completely crazy," the sheriff said. "But unfortunately the law says Annie Bananie has to appear in court."

"Any judge will see Annie didn't do any of that nonsense," Mrs. Johnson said. "The girls didn't even go back to the Bowers' after that one day. Isn't that right, Libby?''

"Uh-huh," Libby said.

"I'm hoping it will be okay with you if Libby comes to court as Annie's witness," Joy said to Mrs. Johnson.

Carl came into the room. "Wow!" he said when he saw the sheriff. "Is somebody a suspect?"

"You, dear," Mrs. Johnson said, walking Carl to the door. "I suspect you need some fresh air."

"No I don't," Carl said, starting down the driveway.

"Meow." Bonnie pranced in front of him. "Is Libby home?"

"Yeah, but she's not allowed out right now," Carl said.

"How come?" Bonnie purred. "Is she grounded?"

"Not exactly," Carl said, walking down the street toward the sheriff's car. "You just better not go to my house right now."

"Meow, I won't," Bonnie said. Then she crept up the walkway to the Johnsons' house and hid in the bushes underneath the window.

"I wanted the sheriff to see what nice girls you and Annie are," Joy said to Libby inside the house.

"I agree," Mrs. Johnson said.

"Because Annie's underage, she can have a lawyer in court," the sheriff said. "Your lawyer will ask some questions before you have to go in front of the judge."

"Like what?" Grandma Gert asked, walking into the room. "I'm the grandmother. I know everything."

"Well, Libby, did you and Annie Bananie do anything to bother the Bowers on the afternoon of the twenty-first?"

"Well, let me think," Libby said. "I—"

"Monday?" Grandma Gert interrupted.

41

"Libby didn't see anything. I can vouch for her. In fact, I remember that Libby came into the house to tell me what she and Annie were going to do."

"Do you remember what she said?" the sheriff asked. "That could be important."

"Of course I do," Grandma Gert said. "Every word. I was taking a little nap. Then Libby said, "Grandma, I'm going with Annie Bananie to rob banks.""

Bonnie was still hiding underneath the Johnsons' window.

"Oh my gosh," she whispered to herself. "They're bank robbers! Wait until everybody hears this!"

Chapter 7

" Okay, cowpokes," Mrs. Liebling said in class the next morning. "Pass your homework up to the front, please."

Annie Bananie took an envelope out of her notebook and brought it up to Mrs. Liebling's desk.

"That's your homework?" Michael Chang asked.

"No, it's a private letter," Annie Bananie said.

"What does it say?" Eddie asked, scratching his head.

"I bet I know what it says," Bonnie said.

"It says Annie Bananie has to miss school because she broke the law."

"No she didn't," Libby said.

"Meow," Bonnie said, smiling at Libby. "I saw the sheriff at your house. I heard everything!"

"Neigh," Nina said. "The sheriff was at your house? Was he on a horse?"

"Did he make you wear handcuffs?" Michael asked.

"No," Libby said. "I'm not a criminal."

"I bet you had to bring a letter, too," Bonnie said, and hissed at Libby.

"Maybe yes, maybe no," Libby said.

"Meow, whatever," Bonnie said. "I know where you guys are going. To court! You're bank robbers!"

Annie's face turned red. Then she jumped up and pulled Bonnie out of her chair to the floor.

"Whoa, Annie Bandito!" Calvin said, moving out of Annie's way.

"That's enough!" Mrs. Liebling said, pulling Annie and Bonnie apart. "What's going on here? What is this all about?"

"I don't believe you," Annie Bananie said to Bonnie. "Why did you have to tell everybody? *I* wanted to!"

"Tell us what?" Mrs. Liebling asked.

"I have to go to court," Annie Bananie said proudly. "My mother and I and Libby's neighbor."

"Oh my gosh, no!" Debbie squealed. "The Bowers?"

"Are you going to jail this time?" Nina asked.

"What are you guys? Like America's Most Wanted?" Eddie asked.

"It says it all in my letter," Annie Bananie said, handing it to Mrs. Liebling. "It's from my mom." Everybody watched Mrs. Liebling's eyes while she read.

"Meow, I'm just glad I was smart enough not to go with Annie," Bonnie said.

"Well, I'll be gosh-darned," Mrs. Liebling said. "You do have to go to court. But not for robbing a bank." She laughed. "You just have a mean neighbor. Are you frightened?"

"Not really," Annie Bananie said.

"Well, you're a brave girl," Mrs. Liebling said, smiling.

"I've got a note from my mom, too," Libby said, handing hers to Mrs. Liebling. "I have to go and be the one and only witness."

"Cool!" Sifredo said, winking at Libby. "Are you going to be on TV?"

"Can I go?" Eddie asked. "You guys are so lucky. This is like a once-in-a-lifetime experience."

"This will be an education for all of us," Mrs. Liebling said. "We can learn a lot from Annie Bananie's and Libby's experience." Annie and Libby smiled at each other.

"Could I be a witness, too?" Bonnie said

to Annie Bananie. "So I made up the thing about the bank robbery. But who was the first person with you who actually saw Mr. Bower's ugly face?"

"Boris!" Annie said, smiling at Bonnie.

"Thanks, but no thanks, Bonnie," Libby said. "I have to be the witness. In fact, Annie Bananie doesn't get to talk. Only I do. There will be a lawyer there with us."

"I can be on the jury," Michael said.

"I know all about the law," Cindy Simon said smartly. "My grandfather is a lawyer. He says in this country you're innocent until proven guilty."

"Very good, Cindy," Mrs. Liebling said.

"Annie Bananie is innocent," Libby said, smiling.

"And my grandfather says the most important thing is you have to tell the truth," Cindy said.

"That's correct," Mrs. Liebling said.

"People who don't tell the truth, the whole truth, and nothing but the truth in court can go to jail."

"That won't happen to me," Libby said quietly.

Chapter

8

"Meow, who's next to see the crime scene?" Bonnie called out. She was sitting at a table in front of Annie Bananie's house. "Twenty-five cents for a tour of the Bowers' house!"

"Do I actually get to go inside?" Eddie asked, scratching his head.

"What are you, crazy?" Bonnie asked. "You might not come out alive. *Tour* is just an expression. Debbie will take you over there. You'll see they always have their curtains closed. You'll get to go into Libby's backyard. You can see the Bowers' backyard from there.

That's where the Bowers said Annie brought Boris's dog poop."

"Do I get my money back if I step in it?" Calvin asked.

"Meow, no," Bonnie said. "But if you want a glass of lemonade, that's an extra ten cents. Hurry up, Nina!"

"Neigh," Nina said, trotting up Annie's driveway with a pitcher and cups. Just then Libby came out of Annie Bananie's house.

"Oink—my gosh," Debbie called out. "Here comes the witness!"

Everybody rushed up to Libby. "What happened in there?" Debbie asked.

"Did that lawyer guy make you confess?" Calvin asked.

"It wasn't so bad," Libby said, trying not to brag. "He just asked Annie Bananie and me a lot of questions. We had to tell him what really happened."

"Cool!" Calvin said. "Like what?"

"Annie Bananie said Mr. Bower wears a wig," Libby said, giggling.

"Did she see it come off?" Nina asked.

"A guy who wears a wig?" Michael asked.

"Who cares about that stuff?" Eddie asked, scratching his head. "Did the lawyer say what happens if Annie goes to prison?"

"No comment," Libby said, trying to walk through the crowd.

"Can you get us a tour inside there?" Sifredo asked. He winked at Libby.

"Oh, man, that would be awesome!" Calvin said. "How much?"

"Meow, what would you want to go in there for?" Bonnie asked. "All you'll get to see is somebody who's going to jail."

"Annie Bananie is not going to jail," Libby said to Bonnie. "If you knew anything, you'd know this isn't that kind of a court thing."

"You think you're the brain of the century," Bonnie said to Libby. "But I know Annie Bananie. She could be a criminal."

"Could not," Debbie said.

"Could so," Bonnie said, and hissed.

"Could not!" Libby shouted.

"Neigh," Nina said, drinking the lemonade from the pitcher.

Just then Annie Bananie's front door opened and Annie came out with Boris and the lawer, Mr. Murphy.

"Oh my gosh," Debbie squealed, "it's them! Can I have your autograph?" Debbie asked Mr. Murphy.

"Who's got a piece of paper?" Calvin asked.

"Can you just sign my hand?" Eddie asked Mr. Murphy.

"Annie Bananie, Boris, and Libby are the celebrities," Mr. Murphy said.

"Sign my hand, too, Annie," Sifredo said,

winking. "This is going to be worth something someday."

"Is your car a limousine?" Nina asked Mr. Murphy.

"No," Mr. Murphy said with a laugh.

"But when Annie Bananie goes to court tomorrow, does she get to go in a limousine?" Calvin asked.

"No, I'm afraid everybody just travels like regular people," Mr. Murphy said as he got into his car.

"Good-bye!" Annie said, waving to Mr. Murphy. "See you tomorrow."

"Meow, so now who's ready for my tour?" Bonnie asked.

"Can we go inside your house, Annie Bananie?" Eddie asked.

Just then Annie's and Libby's mother walked out of Annie Bananie's house.

"Is somebody having a party?" Mrs. Johnson asked.

"Meow, hello, Joy. Hello, Mrs. Johnson,"

Bonnie purred. "Can we go on a tour of your house?"

"Not now," Joy said, laughing. "Annie and I have to go out, and we won't be home until after dinner."

"Come on, Boris," Annie Bananie called, rolling her eyes. "If you want to ride in the car you have to heel." Boris rolled in the grass.

"He doesn't want to heel because he doesn't have his best bandanna," Annie Bananie said to Libby.

"We did good," Annie Bananie whispered to Libby. "We told them everything that happened in the Bowers' backyard. You're going to be the best witness."

"Do you think maybe we should have said Mr. Bower followed us in his car?" Libby asked.

"I told you I wouldn't," Annie Bananie said. "Remember? You said you'd get into trouble. I promised. We're best friends."

"I know," Libby said.

Annie Bananie got into the car with her mother and Boris.

"I didn't tell that Boris lost his best bandanna, either," Annie said. "Don't worry," she whispered to Libby. "We didn't do anything wrong. I'm not afraid. Are you?"

"I'm not so afraid," Libby said as Annie and her mother started to drive away.

Everybody watched Libby and her mother walk back to their house.

"Have I told you how much I love you, Cookie Pie?" Mrs. Johnson asked Libby.

"How come?" Libby asked, smiling.

"Because you're a wonderful young woman. You told Mr. Murphy everything that happened with Boris and going into the Bowers' yard. You couldn't help what Boris did. And you can't help it that the Bowers are the impossible people they are. Telling the truth takes courage. I'm proud of you."

"It's no big deal," Libby said softly, taking

her mother's hand. They crossed the street. Libby saw Mr. Bower walking across his lawn with the poodle.

"You keep your daughter and that Annie Bananie girl away from me," Mr. Bower called out.

"Don't you talk to me or my daughter," Mrs. Johnson called back. Just then Grandma Gert came outside.

"Just talk to the lawyers," Grandma Gert shouted. "And maybe a psychiatrist would be good, too."

"I'll see you in court tomorrow," Mr. Bower said. "Annie Bananie is a menace to society.

"You know what happened, Libby Johnson," he shouted, getting into his car. "And I've got the evidence to prove it." Then he drove away. Libby's hand was shaking.

"Aggh, Libby," Grandma Gert said. "What evidence? Don't you worry about a thing. I'm not going to let anybody hurt you."

"Meow, hello!" Bonnie called from the driveway. "Can I talk to Libby for just a minute?"

"Can I?" Libby asked her mother.

"Okay," Mrs. Johnson said, walking into the house with Grandma Gert. "But dinner is in a half hour."

"What do you want?" Libby asked Bonnie. "No tours."

"I know," Bonnie said. "I wish Annie Bananie never saw the Bowers' house." Bonnie purred softly. Then she started to cry.

"Don't cry, Bonnie," Libby said, putting her arm around Bonnie.

"Meow, I can't help it," Bonnie said. "I'm afraid something terrible is going to happen to Annie Bananie."

"Nothing that bad will happen," Libby said. "The worst thing would be Annie would

have to stay away from the Bowers' house. That would mean she might never want to come to *my* house again."

"Are you sure?" Bonnie asked, crying harder. "Do you promise Annie won't go to prison for life?"

"I'm sure," Libby said. "I promise."

"You're a good friend," Bonnie said, trying to catch her breath. Then she pranced back to her house.

Chapter 9

Libby still had twenty minutes before dinner, so she decided to take a ride on her bike. Barry Avenue was quiet. Nobody was in sight. Libby rode past Bonnie's and Nina's and Debbie's and then back around past Annie Bananie's. Libby thought about what it would be like if Annie Bananie could never come to her house again. She thought about what it would be like being the witness. She turned the corner. Then she started to cry. She pedaled as fast as she could. By the time she got back on her street she was crying so hard, she could barely see. She made out her house ahead. Then she saw something she couldn't believe was real.

Mrs. Bower was sitting on her porch in a lawn chair reading the newspaper. Mr. Bower's car wasn't in the driveway, so Libby knew he wasn't home. Libby had never seen Mrs. Bower sitting outside before. Libby slowed down as much as she could to get an extra-good look. Then she lost her balance and fell onto the Bowers' lawn.

"Who's that?" Mrs. Bower called.

"I'm sorry," Libby said, picking herself and her bike up as fast as she could. "It's me. Libby Johnson. I didn't mean to go on your property. Honest."

Mrs. Bower put down her newspaper. "That's all right, dear," she said. "Please, come here."

Mrs. Bower motioned with one finger for Libby to come over to her. Libby looked over at her own house to see if anyone was watching. Then she started up the Bowers' walk.

She could hardly see Mrs. Bower's eyes behind her thick glasses.

"Hello," Mrs. Bower said, picking up her newspaper again. "Do you like the funnies?"

"Uh-huh," Libby said.

"Could you read this one for me, please?" Mrs. Bower asked, pointing to a comic strip.

"I guess," Libby said.

"Come closer," Mrs. Bower said. "Don't be afraid."

"It says, 'All's well that ends well,' " Libby read.

"That's a pretty funny one," Mrs. Bower said, chuckling. "Thank you for reading to me. I wish I had better eyes. I can't see things up close, and I can't see much far away."

"I understand," Libby said. "My friend Debbie has to wear glasses sometimes, too. She's a very nice girl."

"Uh-huh," Mrs. Bower said, looking at Libby.

"Annie Bananie is a nice girl, too. I think

63

she's probably my nicest friend," Libby said. "You would really like her and Boris if you got to know them. Everybody likes them."

"Uh-huh," Mrs. Bower said. "I had a friend named Annie when I was a girl."

"That's why Annie Bananie really shouldn't have to go to court tomorrow," Libby said.

"I don't know much about these things," Mrs. Bower said.

"I'm the witness," Libby said. "Annie Bananie and Boris will never go near your house again. I promise. Do you think you could get Mr. Bower to change his mind?"

"Change his mind?" Mrs. Bower said. "Oh no, I couldn't do that. I could never tell my husband what to do."

"But couldn't you just ask?" Libby asked. "Mr. Bower knows the truth. And in court you have to tell the truth, the whole truth, and nothing but the truth. Besides, the lawyer says you're never going to win, anyway. I'm the special witness."

"You're a nice girl," Mrs. Bower said to Libby. "I don't know much about these things. But I do know my husband has a witness, too. And he has evidence. I wish I could help you. But my husband says there's no way he's going to lose tomorrow."

"Oh," Libby said, walking slowly backward. Then she picked up her bike and ran home.

Chapter
10

"So? Which case do I hear next?" the judge mumbled in court the next day.

"Bower vs. Bananie, Your Honor," a court clerk called, handing the judge a file.

"That's us," Mr. Murphy said to Annie. "You just leave everything to me. Remember? Libby and I do all the talking. You're not afraid, are you?"

"I'm not so afraid," Annie Bananie said, reaching for her mother's hand.

"Me neither," Libby whispered. Her leg was jumping up and down. Mr. Murphy and Mr. Bower walked up to the judge's bench.

"How does Ms. Bananie plead to the charges?" the judge asked.

"Not guilty, Your Honor," Mr. Murphy answered.

"Oh, she's guilty, all right," Mr. Bower said. "I have evidence right here. For starters, I wrote down every day she came to my house. And she brought Boris, too. Believe me, Your Honor, he's trained to kill."

"Who is this Boris person?" the judge asked.

"Boris isn't a person," Annie called out from her chair. "Boris is my dog!" The people in the courtroom started to laugh.

"Order in the court," the judge said. "Counsel, please advise Ms. Bananie she's not to answer any questions. She's a minor and the defendant."

"I'm sorry," Annie Bananie said. "I forgot."

"Your Honor," Mr. Murphy said, "with

the court's permission, may I please call a witness?"

"All right," the judge said, rubbing her eyes. "But make it snappy."

"Thank you, Your Honor," Mr. Murphy said. "Libby," he called out. "Libby Johnson."

"Go ahead, Cookie Pie," Mrs. Johnson said, giving Libby a hug. "All you have to do is tell the truth."

"Don't be afraid of old Bower-breath," Annie Bananie whispered to Libby. But Libby didn't hear what either of them said. She just walked. Mr. Murphy seemed far away, and the judge's bench looked high up off the ground.

"Hello, Libby," Mr. Murphy said. "All you have to do is answer a few of my questions. Do you understand?"

"Mmm-hmmm," Libby said. Her mouth was so dry, she was afraid she couldn't speak.

"Are you and Annie Bananie friends?"

"Yes," Libby said, looking back at Annie. "We're best friends."

"Very good," the lawyer said. "Did Annie Bananie tell you she wanted to steal anything from the Bowers?"

"No," Libby said.

"And did you hear Annie tell Boris to hurt Mr. Bower? Did she ever say mean things to Mr. Bower or tell you anything bad about him?" Libby turned and looked at Annie. Libby's heart was beating fast.

"Once she said Mr. Bower wears a wig," Libby said. Everyone in the courtroom started to laugh.

"This is ridiculous," Mr. Bower said, touching his hair. "She's the girl's best friend. Of course little girls are going to lie for their best friends."

"I'm not going to lie," Libby said.

"Thank you, Libby," Mr. Murphy said. "You may be seated."

Libby turned and walked back to her seat.

Then she stopped. "Excuse me, Ms. Judge," she said, raising her hand.

"What is it?" the judge said, looking down at Libby over her glasses.

"I forgot to say one piece of the truth," Libby said. "Mr. Bower chased Annie Bananie and me in his car one day."

"What?" Annie's mother called out.

"What?" Mr. Bower said, waving his arms. "I would never do a thing like that."

"Yes you did, Mr. Bower," Libby said. "Don't you remember? It was in the alley. We told you it was okay."

"Ugh," Annie Bananie said to herself. Then she slapped her hand against her forehead.

"I was the one who told Mr. Bower he could chase us," Annie Bananie called out. "But I didn't think he'd really do it. You can send me to jail if you have to."

"You can send *me* to jail if you have to," Libby said to the judge.

"Order in the court," the judge said. "Thank you, Ms. Johnson. You may be seated."

"Your Honor," Mr. Bower said quickly. "These girls have active imaginations. But I have the hard evidence."

"That's okay, Mr. Bower," the judge said. "I've heard enough."

"Your Honor," Mr. Bower said quickly, "what about my case of the dog excrement?"

"And just how do you know the droppings on your lawn belonged to Annie's dog, What's-his-name?" the judge asked, looking through her file.

"She brought them over!" Mr. Bower said. "They were extra-large poops. If I brought one you would see, Your Honor. They're much bigger than my little Weenie could possibly make."

"You have too much time on your hands,

Mr. Bower," the judge said. "But the court doesn't. I've heard enough."

"I have a witness who saw everything," Mr. Bower shouted. "My witness has the hard evidence. I have the right to have a witness, too. May I have one more minute?"

"All right," the judge said. "Make it snappy."

"Quick!" Mr. Bower called out. Everyone turned to look at the back of the courtroom. Mrs. Bower was sitting in the last row. She stood up and started walking slowly toward the front of the room.

"Hurry, Mother!" Mr. Bower said.

Mrs. Bower was all dressed up. Her thick glasses shined in the light. She was carrying a small bag.

"I saw everything, Your Honor," Mrs. Bower said.

"Show them what's in the bag," Mr.

Bower said to Mrs. Bower. "Your Honor," Mr. Bower said, "in this bag are exhibits A, B, and C. A is the stone Libby Johnson left on my lawn when she first tried to kidnap my dog."

Mrs. Bower reached into the bag and lifted out the stone.

"B is the badminton birdie," Mr. Bower said. "The girls hit it into my yard just to see if I was home."

Mrs. Bower lifted the birdie out of the bag and showed it to the court.

"And C," Mr. Bower said with a smile, "is the most important piece of evidence. It's proof that the dog came to my house. Because after he attacked my dog, his scarf fell off."

"Boris's best bandanna!" Annie Bananie called out. Mrs. Bower reached into the bag. There was nothing in it.

"Where's that bandanna, Mother?" Mr. Bower asked.

"I don't know," Mrs. Bower said, looking into the bag. "I can't see it in here."

"What do you mean you can't see it?" Mr. Bower asked.

"Okay, that's enough," the judge said without looking up. "Somebody show Mrs. Bower to a chair. Bower, Annie Bananie, and the girl's guardian and counsel, step forward."

Annie and her mother walked to the judge's bench. Libby's leg was jumping up and down. The judge stamped papers on her desk. Then she looked down at Annie Bananie.

"Mr. Bower," the judge said. "You're asking that Annie Bananie be kept at least a hundred feet from your property. Is that right?"

"That's right, Your Honor," Mr. Bower said.

"And you are asking that the defendant, Annie Bananie's guardian, pay you two thousand dollars for your trouble. Is that right?"

"Yes," Mr. Bower said, smiling. "Or maybe a little bit more."

"Fine," the judge said. "I hereby order that you get nothing."

"What?" Mr. Bower asked.

"Well, maybe not nothing," the judge said. "I'll give you a warning. I don't ever want to see you in my courtroom again. Do you understand?"

Annie's mother gave her a hug. Libby and Mrs. Johnson hugged, too.

"What about that girl?" Mr. Bower shouted.

"Don't you worry about her," the judge said. "I'll take care of her. Go home. Take Mrs. Bower and your dog and go out and get a life. Learn how to live in your community. And by the way," the judge said, "if you ever so much as drive anywhere close to these girls again, I'll throw you in jail so fast your hair will curl."

"I have rights!" Mr. Bower called as he

and Mrs. Bower left the room. Mrs. Bower looked at Libby.

"Step forward, young lady," the judge said to Annie.

"Do I have to go to prison?" Annie Bananie asked.

"Not today." The judge smiled. "There is no case against you. But next time you and Libby and Boris are bored, I suggest you find somebody else to visit. Stay away from the Bowers."

"Don't worry," Annie Bananie said in her friendliest voice. "I won't even go back to find Boris's bandanna. Besides, why would I want to play with somebody who doesn't want to be friendly?"

"Good question," the judge said without looking up. "Now I have one more. What kind of a name is Annie Bananie?"

"It's my real name," Annie said. "I made it up. It's legal."

"I'll take your word for it," the judge said,

trying not to smile. "Remember, it's not legal to chase or follow somebody in a car. If Mr. Bower ever does that again or does anything to bother you, you tell an adult. That's a court order. Okay?"

"Okay," Annie Bananie and Libby said together.

"Good," the judge said. "You girls can go back to school now."

"Do we have to?" Annie asked. "It's almost two o'clock anyway."

"So it is," the judge said, looking at her watch. "I order you girls not to go back to school now. You've had enough education for one day. That is, if it's okay with your mothers."

"It's fine with me," Mrs. Johnson said.

"Let's all get some ice cream," Annie's mother said.

"All right, so who's next?" the judge called out into the courtroom. "What case do I hear now? Let's make it snappy!"

Chapter

11

"Carl, do you mind?" Libby yelled. "I'm trying to tell Grandma what happened today!"

Carl was playing the piano. "What are you, deaf?" Libby yelled louder.

"Aggh, Libby," Grandma Gert said, holding her ears. "I hear every word. Tell me more."

"Then almost the whole class came to Annie Bananie's house after they got out of school. Her mother bought about a thousand dollars of ice cream. Everybody said Annie and I are their heroes!"

"Even the one who thinks she's a cat?" Grandma Gert asked.

"Even Bonnie," Libby said, laughing.

"I'm glad you finally had the courage to tell that Mr. Bower chased you," Grandma Gert said. "It's too bad Bower didn't have the courage to admit it. But believe me, the truth will catch up with him."

"Are you mad we told Mr. Bower to chase us?" Libby asked.

"Not really," Grandma Gert said. "We all say stupid things we don't really mean once in our life. You're lucky that stupid thing didn't cost you. Besides, I knew that very day you were going to get into trouble."

"You did? How?" Libby asked.

"I'm your grandma," Grandma Gert said. "I know everything. And right now I know your mother's trying to put the baby to sleep. Then your father will be home. So I better start making our dinner."

"Hello!" Annie called from outside. "Can I come in? I don't have Boris!"

"Sure," Libby called, running to the door.

"Hello, Grandma Gert," Annie Bananie said in her friendliest voice. "Can Libby play outside until dinner?"

"I won't get into trouble, Grandma," Libby said. "I promise."

"We're just going to run around," Annie Bananie said. "Want to come with us?" she asked, giggling.

"Not today, Annie," Grandma Gert said, laughing. "If I run around I'll drop dead of a heart attack. But as long as you're running, take the garbage out to the alley, will you?"

Grandma Gert handed Annie the trash. Libby and Annie Bananie ran through the backyard. They didn't once look over at the Bowers' yard, but they could tell Mr. Bower wasn't out there. It was quiet outside, and the sun was just starting to go down.

Libby and Annie Bananie stepped into the

alley. Then they froze. Mr. Bower was there, putting the lid on his garbage can.

"Let's go, Libby," Annie Bananie said, stepping back into Libby's yard. "We don't want to get into trouble."

"You don't?" Mr. Bower asked, moving closer. "You think you're out of trouble now? You haven't seen the last of me. I'll take my case to the Supreme Court." He swung his long arms as he spoke. Then he followed Annie and Libby into Libby's yard.

Libby looked over at her house. She wanted to call for help, but she thought nobody would hear her. Suddenly she saw something she couldn't believe. Grandma Gert was running through the yard. And she was running fast.

"Get away from my granddaughter," Grandma Gert hollered. "Don't you dare raise a hand to my girls!"

"Don't run, Grandma," Libby cried. "Please!"

Mr. Bower walked backward into his yard.

"That's right," Grandma Gert said. "Back off! You're giving me a heart attack. You don't know how lucky you are I didn't see you chase my girls in your car! Do you know what I would have done?" she yelled. Grandma Gert stopped. Her face turned bright red.

"Aggh," she said, catching her breath. Then she turned and chased Mr. Bower into his yard.

"You're breaking the law," Mr. Bower said, running.

"So take me to court," Grandma Gert said.

"Grandma, stop! Please!" Libby called.

"Stop, Grandma Gert!" Annie called. "Don't run!"

Grandma Gert chased Mr. Bower in a circle. He ran as fast as he could toward his house.

"Mother!" he called. "Call 911!"

Grandma Gert reached out. She was just

about to grab Mr. Bower by the shirt when something happened. Mr. Bower's wig started to slip. Before he could stop it, the wig flew off his head. Grandma Gert ran right over it. Then she stopped.

Mr. Bower covered his bald head with his hands. Grandma Gert put her foot down on the wig.

"You're standing on my property," Mr. Bower shouted. "Believe me, I'm warning you. My wife is calling 911 right now."

"Let her," Grandma Gert said. "Believe you me, you'll need more than 911 if you ever bother us again! And I think you're also going to need a new wig." Grandma Gert lifted her shoe. "Aggh," she said. "I thought so. Dog poop."

She kicked the wig to Mr. Bower. Mr. Bower grabbed it by one hair and ran into his house.

"Let's go, girls," Grandma Gert said, putting her arms around them.

"Grandma, are you okay?" Libby asked.

"Why shouldn't I be okay?" Grandma Gert asked. "You think the worst thing that ever happened to me is I got a little dog poop on my shoe?"

"That was incredible, Grandma Gert," Annie Bananie said, laughing. "You're my hero!"

"Mine, too, Grandma," Libby said.

Annie Bananie and Libby looked up and saw Mrs. Bower standing in her window. Mrs. Bower opened the window and tossed something out. It was Boris's bandanna.

"This is from Weenie," Mrs. Bower said softly. "It's for Boris."

Annie Bananie ran to pick up the bandanna. Libby couldn't see Mrs. Bower's eyes, but she could tell that Mrs. Bower was smiling.

"Aggh," Grandma Gert said to Libby. "I left the dinner cooking! I hope it doesn't burn the kitchen down! Tonight's a celebration."

"Can Annie Bananie stay for dinner?" Libby asked.

"It's okay with me," Grandma Gert said. "But no dog! We're going to have a special celebration feast."

"What are we having?" Libby asked.

"How about a Weenie roast?" Grandma Gert asked. Then she ran toward the house.

About the Author

Leah Komaiko is the author of many popular children's books, including the bestselling *Annie Bananie, Annie Bananie Moves to Barry Avenue, Annie Bananie—Best Friends to the End,* and *Aunt Elaine Does the Dance from Spain.* This is her third Annie Bananie chapter book and her seventh book for Delacorte Press. She lives in Los Angeles.